Jennifer Adam

HER

Salamander Street

PLAYS

First published in 2024 by Salamander Street Ltd., a Wordville imprint. (info@salamanderstreet.com).

Cover image by Michelle Thompson.

ISBN: 9781068696268

10 9 8 7 6 5 4 3 2 1

Further copies of this publication can be purchased from
www.salamanderstreet.com

"If you have an opinion
Maybe you should shove it
Or maybe, you could scream it... "

This is Why, Paramore

INTRODUCTION

HER is the second play commissioned by Strange Town as part of *The Future is Unwritten*, a programme of new plays for young audiences, funded by Thrive Edinburgh. The other two are *Storm Lantern* by Duncan Kidd and *And...And...And* by Isla Cowan.

These three plays were created to take theatre directly to young people in secondary schools, to kick start conversations and discussion and to pose difficult questions. They are designed to tour and to be of the highest professional standards so that they can be performed in theatres as well as schools.

The first tour of *HER* took place between January–February 2023. It toured to ten secondary schools in Edinburgh and had two public performances at the Scottish Storytelling Centre.

The response to the first tour of *HER* was so positive that we revived the production and toured it again in September–October 2024 with three public performances at Summerhall.

"I have never seen anything like that before. It was amazing"

Feedback from a pupil

Following the performances the company answered questions from the audience.

The idea for *HER* happened after I read a newspaper article about Soma Sara and the 'Everyone's Invited' website. I was appalled and intrigued by the story. How could we begin to talk to young people in schools about what was going on? Having worked with Jennifer Adam before on *Balisong* I knew she'd rise to the challenge of writing this play. Difficult but important conversations around this subject need to be had and theatre is uniquely able to do this.

Steve Small
Producer/Director
Sept 2024

"This show deserves to be seen by as many young people as possible"

Audience member from a public performance

JENNIFER ADAM

Jennifer is an award-winning Scottish Playwright, her play *Walk a Mile* was one of five plays that won the Scottish Short Play Award in 2017.

HER is Jennifer's second play to be commissioned by Strange Town Theatre Company. She was commissioned to write the play *Balisong* about knife crime and active citizenship with Strange Town Theatre in partnership with Fast Forward and No Knives Better Lives. *Balisong* has since been recommissioned twice, touring schools across every local authority in Scotland between 2017 and 2019. The show was seen by 44,000 young people at 225 performances. Both plays were published by Salamander Street.

Jennifer is the Co-Founder of the Tandem Writing Collective, a female-led scratch theatre company which has produced 55 short plays at 20 events since 2016. As one of three playwrights who make up Tandem, Jennifer has written 19 of these short plays, directed two of them and co-produced all 55.

Jennifer has written two plays for the Edinburgh Just Festival as part of the Edinburgh Fringe with Black Dingo Productions, one of which, *Warrior*, went on to tour in two separate school runs funded by Nil by Mouth and Sense over Sectarianism. *Warrior* also received a run at the Citizen's Theatre in Glasgow.

Jennifer has written a number of short plays, working with Strange Town Theatre Company, Scottish Mental Health Arts Festival, A Play, A Pie and A Pint, Tron Theatre, Moonfly Theatre Company, In Motion Theatre Company, Braw Fox Theatre Company, Discover 21 and Village Pub Theatre. She has also written a short radio play, *Looped*, for BBC Radio Drama.

Jennifer was shortlisted for the Tron Theatre's Mayfesto Award in 2019 and was one of the Playwrights' Studio Scotland's mentored playwrights in 2017.

The first performance of *HER* took place on 26th January 2023 at Edinburgh Academy with the following cast:

HER:	**Eleanor McMahon**
HIM:	**Reno Cole**
B1:	**Zara-Louise Kennedy**
B2:	**Edward Hutchings**
Director	**Steve Small**
Designer	**Katie Innes**
Lighting Designer	**George Cort**
Video Designer	**Ellie Thompson**
Sound Designer	**Fi Johnston**
Assistant Director	**Debi Pirie**
Production Manager	**Vanessa Lee**
Stage Manager	**Susan McWhirter**

HER was revived for a new production in September 2024 with the same cast. The creative team was:

Director	**Steve Small**
Designer	**Katie Innes**
Lighting Designer	**George Cort**
Video Designer	**Ellie Thompson**
Sound Designer	**Fi Johnston**
Production Manager	**Scott Ringan**
Stage Manager	**Sam Wilson**

HER was written by Jennifer Adam and commissioned and produced by Strange Town. *HER* is the second play commissioned by Strange Town as part of *The Future is Unwritten*, a programme of new plays for young audiences.

For further information about Strange Town visit www.strangetown.org.uk

CAST

Reno Cole | HIM

Reno is reprising his role as HIM in *HER*, having toured the show in 2023. Other theatre credits include *Takin' Over The Asylum*, *Thebans* and *Macbeth* (Royal Conservatoire Scotland). Screen credits include the lead in *I See Good In Your Eyes* (London Film School), *Outlander* (Sony/Leftbank), *Dash* (Blazing Griffin for BBC Scotland), *Logan High* (Chalkboard TV for BBC) *Tempo* (Screen Education Edinburgh), *Them Upstairs* (Mark Buckland) and *Group* (Pirate Productions). Reno trained at the Royal Conservatoire Scotland.

Edward Hutchings | Bystander 2

Edward is reprising his role as B2 in *HER*, having toured the show in 2023. Other theatre credits include *The Other Way Home* (New Diorama/Kandinsky), *Muster Station: Leith* (R&D, Grid Iron), and *Mary Slessor* (Scotland's History Festival). Screen credits include *Logan High* (Chalkboard TV for BBC iPlayer), *The Funeral* (Screen Education Edinburgh), and various commercials and music videos. Edward began acting in youth theatre and performed in various productions of new writing in Scottish venues such as the Traverse Theatre and the Netherbow, Edinburgh. He trained at Performing Arts Studio Scotland.

Zara-Louise Kennedy | Bystander 1

Zara-Louise Kennedy is an Edinburgh-based actor, originally from Dumfries & Galloway. Since earning her BA in Acting and English from Edinburgh Napier University in 2022, Zara-Louise has gone on to tour with, koi collective and Strange Town Touring Company, where she performed in the 2023 production of Jennifer Adam's *HER*. She has also starred in short films, including *Coldsores* and *Waiting For Marcus*. In addition to on-screen and stage, Zara-Louise continues to lend her voice to many Scottish VO projects such as Bright Bus Tours and Trust Care. Having just performed in *Hysterical* (koi collective) by Sally MacAlister at Edinburgh Fringe 2024, Zara-Louise is thrilled to be reprising her role in *HER* with Strange Town Touring Company.

Eleanor McMahon | HER

Eleanor is a Scottish actor and writer based in Edinburgh. She graduated from Edinburgh Napier's Acting and English course in 2021. Her stage credits include, *The Clink* (New Celts), *Saving Mr Ultimate* (Extra Arca and New Celts), *Love And Information* (New Celts), *Chicago, Chicago!* (Name Pending Entertainment), *HER* (Strange Town) and *The Ugly Duckling* (Folksy Theatre). Her film credits include *Levelling Up* (Zigstar Productions) and *Simon Says* (Champdog Films). She is passionate about feminist and queer theatre and is excited to be touring again with Strange Town and reprising her role in *HER*.

CREATIVE TEAM

Steve Small | Director / Producer

Directing credits for Strange Town include: *Storm Lantern* by Duncan Kidd—Traverse Theatre and Edinburgh schools tour May-June '24 & Scottish Storytelling Centre & Edinburgh schools tour Sept/Oct '22, *And... And... And* by Isla Cowan—Traverse Theatre & Edinburgh schools tour Sept/Oct '23, Original tour of *HER* by Jennifer Adam—Scottish Storytelling Centre & Edinburgh schools tour Jan/Feb '23, *Balisong* by Jennifer Adam (in partnership with Fast Forward), toured to every local authority in Scotland from 2017–2019; *Dr Korczak's Example* by David Greig, produced for Holocaust Memorial Day 2018 and at the 2018 & 2019 Edinburgh Festival Fringe and toured secondary schools in Edinburgh, East Lothian and Fife; *A Field Of Our Own* by Duncan Kidd—first sold out show of the 2017 Edinburgh Festival Fringe; *Being A Dad* by Duncan Kidd (in partnership with Fathers' Network Scotland), 2016 Edinburgh Festival Fringe sellout and toured prisons, community centres and conferences.

Storm Lantern was nominated for a 2023 CATS Award for best production for children and young people.

Steve is the Artistic Director & Joint Executive Director of Strange Town.

Katie Innes | Designer

Katie graduated with a BA (hons) Drama and Performance degree from Queen Margaret University, specialising in design and scenic art, further developing her skills on the Scenehouse Design course. As the Design and Production Manager for Strange Town, she works regularly on their youth theatre productions including, during the pandemic, a large-scale, multi-media event *Gen Z*. For the touring company she designed the set and costumes for: *Dr Korczak's Example* by David Greig, *Storm Lantern* by Duncan Kidd, *HER* by Jennifer Adam & *And... And... And* by Isla Cowan. It is Katie's hope that having a motivated, creative, working mum will be an inspiration to her daughters.

George Cort | Lighting Designer

George has been a professional theatre lighting technician and designer for over 15 years. In that time, he has lit dance, musical theatre, opera and drama. Recent credits for Strange Town touring company include *Storm Lantern*, *HER*, *And... And... And*, Strange Town's summer youth theatre shows at the Traverse Theatre as well as *The Gods, The Gods, The Gods* for Wright & Grainger at the Edinburgh Festival Fringe 2022.

Fiona Johnston | Sound Designer

Fi is a freelance sound designer, stage manager and educator based in Glasgow. She trained at what was then the RSAMD 2003-2006, specialising in Sound Design and Stage Management, and then got her MSc Sound Design at The University of Edinburgh in 2007. Recent Collaborators include; National Theatre Scotland, Gary McNair, Janice Parker, untitled projects, The Lyceum Theatre, The Unicorn Theatre, A Moment's Peace, Edinburgh Science Festival, Abu Dhabi Science Festival.

Ellie Thompson |Video Designer

Ellie studied at the Royal Central School of Speech and Drama. After graduating she has worked in various video roles including video supervisor, video programmer, associate designer and video designer for productions.

As Video Designer, theatre includes: *Bluets* (Royal Court Theatre, London); *Black Sheep* (Curious Directive, Norwich); *Through The Mud* (Stellar Quines & Royal Lyceum Theatre); *Lament For Sheku Bayoh* (Royal Lyceum

Theatre, National Theatre of Scotland & Edinburgh International Festival); *HER* (strange Town Touring Company); *Den Kirschgarten—The Cherry Orchard* (Deutsches Schauspielhaus, Hamburg); *Christmas At Inverleith House* (Lightworks); *Meet Jan Black* (Gaiety Theatre; Ayr); *The White Bike* (The Space, London).

Scott Ringan | Production Manager

Scott is an Edinburgh-based freelance Stage Manager. His recent credits include: *The Outrun* (Lyceum Theatre/EIF), *Escaped Alone* (Tron Theatre), *Peter Pan* (Crossroads/Festival Theatre). In 2023 Scott toured America with *The Strange Undoing Of Prudencia Hart* (Lyceum Theatre/Double M) prior to an eight week Off-Broadway run at the McKittrick Hotel. Scott is thrilled to be working once again with Strange Town after successful tours with *Storm Lantern* (2022, 2024) and *And... And... And* (2023).

Samantha Wilson | Stage Manager

Samantha graduated university in 2022 with a BA in Technical Theatre. Since then she has worked on several theatre shows, the most recent include; *Peter Pan's Pantomime Adventures*, *Hamilton* (UK and Ireland Tour) and five Edinburgh Festival Fringe shows including a sold out run with Andrew Frost, one of the worlds leading magicians in card magic.

About Strange Town

Strange Town is a charity that uses theatre and the
arts as a creative catalyst to nurture talent and
increase access to opportunities in the arts for children and young people
based in Edinburgh.

Ruth Hollyman & Steve Small	Joint Executive Directors
Steve Small	Artistic Director
Jessica Chalmers	General Manager
Katie Innes	Design & Production Manager
James Beagon	Youth Theatre Manager
Ruth Hollyman	Agency Director
Ailis Mundin	Agency Assistant
Claire Montgomery	Fund Raiser

Thanks to the following for their help with this production: James
Beagon, Andy Catlin, Katie Fraser, Linda Irvine, Debi Pirie, Michelle
Thompson, Emma Quinn and everyone at Greenside Church.

Supported by: The Backstage Trust, The Foyle Foundation, Nancie Massey
Charitable Trust.

F: strangetownco
Insta: strangetownco
www.strangetown.org.uk

Strange Town is a charity and limited company by guarantee incorporated in
Scotland with company number SC330197 and Scottish charity number SC04564.

We need your help to continue to make these plays available for young people in
Edinburgh. If you're able to donate to help us continue this work, scan the QR
code or visit strangetown.org.uk/donate

HER

A play by Jennifer Adam

CHARACTERS:

HER

Female, 16/17, 5th year pupil, Scottish

HIM

Male, 16/17, 5th year pupil, Scottish

BYSTANDER 1

Female, 16-18, Scottish

BYSTANDER 2

Male, 16-18, Scottish

Ideally, at least one actor will be non-white. As this is a play that is ultimately about equality, it is important that young people of colour are represented in this story and that their experiences of gender inequality—which is often experienced alongside racism or other discrimination of their culture or religion—are referenced. Some lines can be altered to suit that actors' experiences.

BYSTANDER 1 and BYSTANDER 2 will also take on other roles, this should be apparent in the script. This can be conveyed with small props or discrete costume additions/changes.

1. THE INTRO

On stage are five flat boards that act as steps.

The intro/opening of This is Why *by Paramore plays (suggestion: sec 1-8, 31-53, fading out at 30 Seconds.)*

HER is standing at the top of some steps. The rest size her up. Make her uncomfortable. There is an essence of a witch being held at the gallows, being looked upon by villagers.

They circle her. Music stops and they sit. She towers in the middle of them.

HER: I'm Her.
By the way.
The one you heard about.
That's me.
I am she.
I am.
Actually, I don't...
I don't have a name.
I guess..

B1: It's not important

HER: I don't have an actual name.
Like you do

B2: Doesn't matter.

HER: But it doesn't change the fact.

B1: All that's important.

B2: All you need to know is...

HER: I am
Her.
She is me.

...

And I know
you've probably formed your own opinion already,
Right?

B1: She sounds posh.

B2: She doesnae look posh.

B1: I mean, haircut from the 90s.

B2: That fringe man.

B1: She's pretty though

B1 and B2 both squint.

 In a relaxed sort of way

B2: She's quiet.

HIM: She never used to be.

B1: Now,
She's quiet.

HIM: Loudest kid in the playground.

B2: Now she's quiet
Because when you're told
you're too loud

B1: You're too much

B2: Too often

B1: Maybe you decide to just...

HER: I get it.
Everyone has an opinion
about me these days

HIM: And as for her hair—
It hasn't changed.
Not in 16 years.

B2: They knew each other before
like, as babies

B1: They were baby pals.

B2: Back when His "original" Dad was still around

B1: Back when they would walk to school hand in hand
Mum to kid to kid to Mum

B2: Like a chain of protection

B1: When both Mums would laugh about how
"one day they might get married."

HIM: And they say time can distort memories,
but I'm certain
If you asked me what she looked like when she was born
Like literally
Head coming out the womb
I reckon I would have said,
Tiny.
Chubby.
...

Ponytail and a blunt fringe.
Seriously.

B1: I like Him, he's funny.

B2: He's really cool.

B1: He's also like buff, but not totally ripped

B2: Yeh, it's cos he does all the sports

B1: My pal Jenny said that Sarah said that Becky said he does all the sciences.
Biology

B2: Chemistry

B1: Physics

B2: ...Is there another one?

B1: If there is, I bet he does that too.

B2: He's proper brainy

B1: Yeh, he's brains and the body

B2: He has all the things.

HER: But the thing is,
Not a lot of people know the truth

B2: Facts is facts.

HIM: Not a lot of people believe
The truth.

B2: Not a lot of people really know Her.

HER: And actually,
I need your help.

HIM: We were inseparable.
Until we weren't.

HER: I need you
To help me.

This request is to the audience, but in the silence afterward HIM and HER's eyes meet, he looks as if he's about to speak. But she's ready to start her story.

2. MONDAY. THE DAY IT HAPPENED

Suggested image on screens across the backdrop: A long consecutive strip of red tape, giving the impression of being barriered in.

HER: It started on Monday.

HER races to the bottom of the steps.

B1: Most weeks usually do.

HER: First thing
Monday morning

B2: Except she doesn't have a first thing Monday morning

HER: Study period

B1: Dunno how much studying goes on

B2: It works for her though, this free Monday morning

B1: Needs the rest after three nights on her feet

HER: Three nights and two full days on my feet

B2: Just to serve to rich folk their dinner

B1: Top up their Pinot Grigio
You wouldnae catch me in there like

B2: They wouldnae let you in

B1: Posh wumin and their pervy husbands

B1 and B2 briefly sit like they're in a restaurant.

B1/WIFE: I'll take the light souffle, with the fat-free cream, wait-ress

B2/HUSBAND: And which lager would you recommend, darlin?

HER: They always ask me that
The men always want my opinion on booze
Like they want to test my knowledge or show off theirs
Even though I'm legally required to wear a badge that announces my age.
Forced to shout about the fact that I'm UNDER 18.

B1: An under 18 Badge.

B2: Uh huh.

B1: That's the opposite of what you want isn't it?

HER: I don't drink, Sir, I tell them
Shrug like it's super unfortunate.

B2/HUSBAND: Away!!! Here, and get one for yourself

HER: And he offers me a £20 note.

B1: She smiles back at him through gritted teeth and says

HER: No thank you.

B1: But he stands,

HER: He towers over me, and forces the money into my hands

HER politely takes the money

B1: Restaurant Manager just standing in the corner laughing about it.

HER: And that is why, come Monday
I'm done.

B1: Seriously

HER: Common Room,

B1: Sofa out.

HER: Cover myself in that moth-ridden blanket
that they Janny maybe washed some time in the last decade
Shut the blind
...And I probably doze off

B2: Probably.

B1: Most likely

B2: Not so difficult when you have something warm to cuddle into though

B1: Not too hard to fall asleep, snuggled into your boyfriend though

B2: Ryan

B1: Ryan's a 6th Year

HIM: Ryan looks about 30.

B2: You know the kinda guy that had a beard in S2?

B1: Hangs about with all the football guys

B2: Too cool to actually play though

HIM: Too cool to do anything

B1: Which is why he skives whatever it is he has every Monday morning

B2: Every Monday
to see Her.

B1: To sit in the common room and (*coughs*) study.

HER: Like I said.
I needed to sleep.

B1 and B2 share a glance.

B1: Bit loud I reckon

B2: The footfall

B1: Bit noisy to try and snooze with all the passersby

B2: Folk coming in, going out, running to class

HIM: There are these stripes along the walls in our school
Red, orange or green tape runs along every corridor
Like a barrier, fencing you in.

B2: It's a traffic light system
Supposed to keep students out of areas they shouldn't be in

B1: Red tape all around the staff room

B2: The back offices

B1: And technicians' lab.

B2: Orange around every route to every classroom,

B1: You can only go in there if you're en route to someplace else

B2: And green for the places you can freely grace with your presence at any time

B1: Canteen.

B2: Locker Area.

B1: Toilets.

HIM: And
the common room.

You see it was meant for 5th and 6th Years
But it was open to anybody with enough balls to go in.

B1: It was a safety thing they said.

B2: Prevent bullying?

HIM: They wanted to make it a safe space.
...
In the end it was so small, barely anybody used it.
Except to sleep.
Apparently.

HIM touches the red tape, there is a clear shift in tone, maybe the lights change

B2: Your brain does this thing sometimes

B1: Makes connections
Even when you don't want it to

B2: Even when you really don't need it to

B1: Sometimes it's foreshadowing something

B2: Sometimes,
It's a trigger.

HIM: It's the red tape that comes away the easiest
Hanging there
Like it's asking to be peeled away

B1: Probably because folk pick at it so much
Scrape it off.

9

B2: So they can go where they like
then plead ignorance

HIM: It's the sticky bit
That's what my brain remembers
That's the bit that hits me in the gut

B2: We see tape,
He sees

HIM: A suitcase

B2: It makes him flashback
To that evening he spent at Her house
Age 8

HIM AND HER sit next to each other like they're on a sofa, aged 8 and glued to the TV. He is wearing a large Marvel cap, too big for his head.

B1: That evening where he sat in her living room for hours watching Batman cartoons on repeat

B2: Scoffing endless packets of Jammy Dodgers

B1: While his Dad packed his things next door
ramming it all into one giant suitcase case

B2: With bits of clothes and random shoelaces
Bursting out the gaps

B1: Refusing to be contained
by red sticky tape

B2: Red sticky tape that He'll try and pry off the case when he gets home

B1:   Red sticky tape under his fingernails
scratch marks down the side of the leather
...

B2: A sudden change of house meant a change of school for Him
And a lonely second half of Primary School for Her

B1: Ach, she made some friends

B2: Wasn't quite the same though.
Not sitting next to him in class.

B1: Not seeing him in the playground

B1: Not walking home together as a link, protected by held hands

10

...

B2: Saw each other every so often,
For a while at least

B1: Until the space between got wider

B2: Until space
Was all that was left

B1: Until High School reunited them

B2: Until PSE and Art and Human Biology reunited them.

B1: It's a lifetime ago for Her,
But for Him,
He sees that red tape

B2: He touches the glue and lets it stick to his skin

B1: And He's right back there,
in that moment.

HIM gets up and walks away, HER watches him leave. HE removes his cap.
Lights go back to normal

B1: Bit of a shame he's got to look at it here every day, eh?

B2 Gestures to the tape

B2: There are a few 'interesting' things about our school to be fair.

B1: Unisex open-plan toilets.

B2: A climbing wall in the courtyard.

B1: Just asking for someone to split their head open.

B2: Ma big sister said that her pal's cousin Ahsan
deliberately threw himself off so he could get out of doing
social dance.

B1: I mean,
I get that.
...
But
One thing we're OK at
is fairness

B2: Overall

B1: The teachers
They're alright, eh?

B2: ...eh ...Aye.

B1: Like,
Miss French.

3. WEDNESDAY: THE DAY IT CAME OUT (PART 1)

Suggested images on screens: Cucumber. Aubergine. Banana.

All four land at their desks.

HER: Jump to Wednesday morning and we're in PSE.
And It's full of girls

B1: Because all the girls like Ms French.

HER: Because nothing is off-topic

B1: Because she treats you like an adult.

HIM/B2: She's awright/She's OK

B1: She'll go from Atheism to Abortion in one lesson

HER: And that's just the As.
Today is Sex Education.

B1: Sex. Ed. You know that class where they teach you about
condoms?
How to open one.
How to put one on.
But not how to insist
boys actually wear one.

HER: Not Miss French
Nothing is off limits
And she struts into the classroom looking like a teenager

B1: But with the confidence of someone who is about to give a
speech at the UN or something!

HER: Because she believes all her lessons
Are that important

B1 dons a pair of on-trend glasses and becomes MISS FRENCH, she walks in front of the class. The boys in the class are on their phones, HER discreetly checks her phone throughout the scene.

HER: She inhales as she pivots at her desk,
Ready to speak the moment she's facing us
and literally in one breath, she says,

FRENCH: Today we're discussing the things you're too
embarrassed to ask about.
And we're starting with
Periods!
Guess what. They happen!
Guys, phones down. We're all going to learn something today.

They all put their phones down. FRENCH turns her back and they immediately bring their phones back out. B1 removes and puts back on her glasses when she moves between being B1 and FRENCH.

B2: He turns it onto silent, but the messages keep coming

HIM: If I don't respond, he just sends more

B1: Even though he's in class

HIM: Even though **he knows** I'm in class

B2: But His current Stepdad-type figure,
He's an interesting one.

HIM: He's like... nice.
...
It's fucking weird.

B2: He texts most mornings, lunchtimes and afternoons

B1: Likes to make sure He's actually turned up to school

B2: Likes to make sure He's OK

HIM: He asks if I'm 'awright'.
Am I 'cool' (*double thumbs up!*)
Aye... I'm 'cool'. Thanks

B2: But it is literally
every day

HIM: I start feeling like I need to make stuff up just for a wee bit of variation.

Ehh aye... throat's a wee bit scratchy today but I think I'll live.

HER checks her phone, nothing.

He laughs. On text.

HA HA HA HA...

Christ, It's like getting messages from Alexa.

B1: I mean,
You can understand the confusion,

B2: The curiosity

B1: This seemingly friendly chap

B2: After a lifetime of older men coming in and out his life

B1: Each one shadier and more stupid than the last

B2: Each one demonstrating their own unique blend of toxic masculinity

B1: Courie-ing up to His Mum while letting Him know who was boss.

B2: They expected Him to take it.
Wee guy 8/9 years old.
They expected him to do what he was told.

B1: And he did, to be fair.
He did what he was told.
Only, before these guys showed up
There were family members

B2: Older aunties mostly
Who gathered him up the day his Daddy left and told him

B1: 'You're the man of this hoose now, son'
'You better look efter that mither ae yours, right?'

B2: 'Big boys dinnae cry, son'
'Man up. Just grow a pair, wid ye?'

B1: His tiny eight-year-old brain trying to figure out...

B2: A pair of what??

B1: And so as expected, even at eight years old
There was a bit of push-back

B2: Started small, but by the time He was in P4,
he'd learned to cry on cue whenever this new boyfriend came
into the room.
So naturally his Mum dumped the guy.

B1: By age ten he'd found the perfect lie

B2: Told his Mum He'd seen her boyfriend coming out Big
Jackie's house .

He nudges HER, directs his lines to HER as if they're back there. She largely ignores HIM, softly reacts.

HIM: All the boys know Big Jackie,
if you know what I mean

B2: And so he too was chucked
faster than a cold chippy

HIM: None of them lasted, not with this guy in town

B1: And by 11 he'd graduated to full-on violence

B2: Turning up at Her house with bruises on his arms and blood
on his knuckles

B1: She didn't ask.
She didn't want to know.

B2: At this point, she barely recognised her pal

B1: I mean, she was worried,
But she was also sick to the back teeth of his bad chat

HIM: She loved it

B2: She really didn't

HIM: She could see that I had become a hero
And that's what everyone wants at the end of the day, eh?
That's what everyone needs in their life.

HIM puts his Marvel hat back on to make a point, but it barely fits, it just sits on his forehead, brief nod to a flashback, HER gets up and comes into this world.

B1: She could see right through Him

B2: She could see the tiny guy she grew up with, buried in there

HER: I want to help you.

HIM snubs/snorts at HER.

B2: Buried underneath all this macho exterior

HER: What do you need?
 Tell me what you need,
 And I'll do it

(Pause.)

B2: And she meant it by the way.
 She really meant that.
 But,

HIM: It's everybody else who needs ME.

B1: And his eyes are darting about like,

HIM: What do you know about life?

B2: And He laughs at Her.

HIM: What do you know about anything??

B1: And all She can think is,

HER: What has actually happened to you?

B2: She'd had enough.

B1: But He kept going,

B2: Kept trying to regale her with more stories,
 More anecdotes

B1: More tales of revenge and vindication until I suppose She snapped

B2: I supposed she'd been holding her tongue for actual months
 Because when He starts talking about another guys she goes...

HER: I've completely lost track which of your Mum's multiple guys you're referring to actually!

(...cawks)

B2: Yeh.
 That'll pretty much end a friendship.

HER fades away back to her seat while HIM removes His Marvel cap. We return to the scene. HIM is still texting. HER's phone is still blank.

The Bell rings.

FRENCH: Good work. Next week we'll be discussing how society
created the conditions
for the holocaust to happen—
So bring your moral compass!

*He approaches HER, as they leave the classroom, HER does't notice and she
walks right by HIM. He watches her walk away.*

B1: Her next class is Art.
But that's not where she's off to.

B2: She races to the opposite end of the building

B1: To the one place in school you where can skive off
and still make it look like you're working if you get caught.

B2: She heads
to the music room.

B1: Guaranteed that's where Ryan will be

B2: He's always in there,
bunking off

B1: hiding out practicing guitar or drums for his band

B2: And those rooms aren't soundproofed by the way

B1: But hey, we never said the guy was clever, alright?

B2: So that's where she goes
after almost 24 hours with zero communication from him

B1: But when she walks in it's full of

HER: Eugh!

B1: First years

B2: They look at Her like a teacher's just walked in
Instantly stand to attention
And the noise falls

B1: And so she turns round to run back to class
But tries to message Ryan again on her way there

B2: So she's not actually looking where she's running

B1: She turns a corner and bumps right into

B2 puts on a pair of clunky glasses, he become YOUNG GUY.

B2/YOUNG GUY
& HER: Sorry!!

B1: They're not friends, just to be clear.
But they're not **not** friends either,
They just happen to have the same surname,
and so were put next to each other in registration.
Side by side, ten minutes a day for five actual years.

YOUNG GUY: You left your book-

HER: My—

YOUNG GUY: Note book—

HER: Right—

YOUNG GUY: It's got all your notes in it—

(He hands it back)

HER: Yeh thanks.

YOUNG GUY: I didn't read it!

HER: OK—

YOUNG GUY: You left it lying—

HER: I was in a—

YOUNG GUY: Hurry, I know. *(He is also out of breath trying to catch her.)*

HER: I'm late for—

YOUNG GUY: I know.

HER smiles at the guy and goes to walk away. YOUNG GUY hesitates, he considers not asking, but,

Are you OK?

HER: *(taken aback)* Yes

YOUNG GUY: I just mean,
after—

HER: After what.

YOUNG GUY: ...I just wanted to check if you were OK.

B1: Does he know things?
It sounds like he knows things.

HER: Why wouldn't I be?

YOUNG GUY: I... I dunno.
...But if you weren't,
Then... I'm here. (He waves at her awkwardly)

HER: ...Good to know.

B1: And they stare at each other
A little longer than is polite, frankly.
Then they remember where they're supposed to be
and they bolt.

HER and B2 disappear in opposite directions. B2 removes his glasses.

4. WEDNESDAY: THE DAY IT CAME OUT (PART 2)

Images on screens: self portraits that eventually move and melt into scarier things.

HIM, B1 and B2 slump down into new seats. They are now in Art class. There are images of bizarre self portraits displayed on the screens above, think Van Gogh inspired, but by teenagers. They become slowly distorted as the scene goes on. HER sneaks in nervously.

B1: So she walks in late to Mr Mullin's Art class.

B2: Has to squeeze past every desk

B1: Every table with a face on it
A duplicate

B2: Self portraits that bear literally no resemblance to the person drawing them

B1: Artistic licensing at its finest

B2: She feels like she's walking passed every single person
Twice

B1: Every pupil plus their distorted reflection
to get to that one free desk

B2: That one at the back

B1: The one by itself

B1: And she snakes her way past

B2: Over bags and around chairs

B1: It's like a maze

B2: A maze with eyes

B1: As if they'd never seen someone walk in to class late before

HER finds a desk and sits. HIM, B1 and B2 sit at their desks and stare at her.

...

B1: She's not having a good day, is she?

B2: And it's about to get worse.
Because that's when it happened

B1: She didn't even have her pen out

B2: Barely opened her book when—

PING!–Her phone.

She jumps and looks. The others wince.

HER is disgusted, but all too familiar with what has been sent. The drawings above start to move.

HER: Something I will never understand.

B1 and B2 put ties on. They are pupils in the class.

B2/PUPIL laughs.

I mean, I'm just sitting here.
Teacher five feet away
And...

PING!

B2/PUPIL: You're welcome!

B1 and B2 laugh.

HER: Like it's right there
No warning,
No filter.

PING!

PUPIL: Different angle this time

HER: Why do you think I'd want to see that?

PUPIL: You love it. (*He makes a biting sound*)

HER: Why would anybody
want to see that?

PUPIL: Because it's funny

HER: Am I laughing?

PUPIL: It's funny to me.

PING!

HER: Just stop!

PUPIL: Why though?

HER: Because I'm asking you to STOP.

PUPIL: You'll like this one

HER: I'm turning my phone off

PING! - this time everyone's phone goes. HIM and B1 look at their phones and react.

PUPIL: Ohhhhh these are good

HIM: Oh God.

HER: Can't see it.

PUPIL: Effortless

HER: Don't care

HIM: Someone take her phone!

PUPIL: You've done this before, eh?

HIM: Someone take it before she sees—

PUPIL: Does she know—

HER: Can't hear you.

PUPIL: I said, HEY!

SHE looks over.

You've done this before.

Haven't you.

SHE looks at her phone, and is horrified.

B1 and B2 stand and move closer and closer to her. They momentarily return to being bystanders. HIM is in the background horrified.

B1: Skin

B2: Legs

B1: Breasts

B2: Blouse

B1: Skirt

B2: Hands

B1: Lips

B2: Shoulders

B1: Skin

B2: Her skin

B1: Her arms

B2: Her underwear

B1: Her bra

B2: Her eyes

B1: Her mouth

B2: Her face

B1: Her face

B1 and B2 slam back down to their desks, we are back in the room.

HIM: It can't be–

B1 PUPIL: It totally is

B2/PUPIL: It definitely is

B1 PUPIL: It's/

HER: /This isn't possible

B2/PUPIL: Oh come on now, shy girl

HER: That can't be—

B1 PUPIL: Probably took those herself

B2/PUPIL: Such an attention seeker

B1 PUPIL: Aw asleep, are ye?

HER: Asleep?

B1 PUPIL: Can literally see your eyeballs
She's totally awake, man

B1 PUPIL: Could have used a filter

B2/PUPIL: Coulda pulled it down a bit
Pushed them up

B1 PUPIL: Flat tits

B2/PUPIL: Look at the way her legs go

B1 PUPIL: Why would you even?

B2/PUPIL: Is that—Can I see her—?

B1 PUPIL: Disgusting,
honestly if I had a body like that I would keep it hidden

HIM: Somebody should help Her

B1 PUPIL: That's her arms

B2/PUPIL: That's her legs, Trust me.

HER: I can't focus

B2/PUPIL: That's right up her skirt

HIM: I kept waiting for somebody to help Her

HER fights to get through the desks and bags, fumbling and falling

HER: I can't breathe

B2/PUPIL: Should be flattered, you're well fit

B1 PUPIL: Yeh, you should be thanking us

23

HIM: And I can see she's terrified
And I want to say something

HER: I can't get out

HIM: But would she thank me for it?
After all this time?
Maybe she did take those pictures?
Maybe she did share them?

HER: I need to leave!

HIM: And I know it sounds bad, but if I say something
If I stick my neck out
Tell them to back off

B1 PUPIL: Ohhhh we've found the photographer!

B2/PUPIL: Make us some porn will ye?

B1 PUPIL: Watch out girls, creeper over here's on snapchat

HIM: You want me to do that?
You want me to go up against them all?

HER & B1: YES

HIM: You want me to put myself in the line of fire??

HER & B1: YES!

HIM: I mean,
That just doesn't sound safe!

B1 and B2 take their ties off

HER manages to get through the maze and runs out the door. She races to the third step and takes out her phone.

B1: And He calls himself a hero

B2: We love to think so, eh?

B1: Thinks He's the big man

B2: We love to think we'll step up when time time comes
but honestly,

HIM: (*defensive*) We're all just trying to survive here!

HER is on the other side of the stage.

HER: It's blurry
And I'm literally shaking
which isn't helping
But I can see in the background of one of the pictures
the faint markings,
a long green line
tape across a wall
the edge of a sofa
... and that moth-ridden blanket.

And suddenly it dawns on me
Why he's not messaged.
All. Day.

So I call him.

HIM, B1 and B2 are on the other side of the stage; they collectively embody RYAN, her boyfriend. They don some kind of douchey clothing/prop to convey they are the same person.

I ring him right then and there
And he actually picks up
he actually has the nerve to say,

ALL 3: Hey babe

HER: I say,
There's photos of me
There's actual pictures
On Snapchat
Of my legs
Of my...

B2: *(Nonchalant bit also a little bit guilty)* Yehhh, Riiiight.

HER: I ask him flat out,
did you take those pictures?
Did you
Unbutton my shirt
Lift up my...
Did you take them on Monday when I was asleep in the common room?
And he goes,

ALL 3: Um... yeh?

HER: Like it's nothing?!
Like I'm overreacting?!

They collectively sigh like they're already bored of her drama.

HIM/RYAN: You let me take a picture of your bra months ago

HER: That's not what this is—

B2: Your face is barely in the others

HIM/RYAN: Can't even tell it's you

B1: It's not my fault the guys found them on my phone

B2: It's not my fault they screenshot them

HIM/RYAN: It's not my fault they ended up on Snapchat

B1: You were obviously into it that first time at my house

HIM/RYAN: You should really be clearer if that's not something you're into any more

B2: Like it's total mixed messages you're giving me right now

HER: Mixed messa—

B1: You want me to ask every single time??

HIM/RYAN: Do you understand how completely unrealistic that is?

B2: I mean, you're supposed to be my girlfriend

ALL: Are you still there?
Hello... ?
UGH

They disperse to signify the end of the call, losing their RYAN prop

B1: And you can see her start to spiral

B2: You can see her it in her eyes
as she obsessively looks back through the images

B1: Trying to find flaws

B2: Trying to find something

B1: Anything

B2: That might prove her wrong

B1: That might make her realise

B2: That actually

B1: That maybe

B2: Those aren't her legs and skirt

B1: Her breasts.

B2: This isn't the Primark bra that got snagged on the side of the washing machine

B1: The one she hasn't replaced because she bought it for him

B2: She bought it because she knew he would see it

B1: Well, now everyone's seen it

B2: But there's no doubting it

B1: You can stare at those pictures all day long
They're not moving

B2: Not changing shape

B1: They won't suddenly melt into someone else.

B2: Her skin was there for everyone to see

B1: Captured,
while she slept.

HER: I have to get out of here.

B1: What, to go home?

HIM: Her Mum's at home
She would understand

B2: I mean
It would be hellish
Having to tell her

B1: Having to go into the details

B2: Especially if she let him take one, months back

B1: But this isn't about that.
This is about Monday.
What Ryan and his friends have done.

B2: Still, cringe

HIM: But she's reasonable isn't she? Her Mum?

B1: She's one of the good ones

B2: Good intentions at least

B1: Except...

HIM: Except...?

B1: There was that TV show they watched

B2: Oh Christ.

B1: One of those shows that you start watching with your parents and then slowly it dawns on you

B2: This is not a programme you want to watch with your parents.

B1: I mean it's bad enough just watching folk kissing on tellie
When your parents are in the room

B2: But this wasn't just kissing

B1: This was like

B2: This was full on

B1: Like totally
Oh my God my Dad is next to me

B2: But the storyline

B1: That episode they watched

B2: That episode they pure sat all the way through

B1: It was a bit like this
Wasn't it?

B2: It was bit similar like

B1: And that guy
He sent his ex's nudes to her pals

B2: Her boss

B1: Her family

B2: Mortifying

B1: They watched this together.
And all Her parents had to say was

B1 and B2 Briefly become her parents.

B1/MUM: I just don't understand

B2/DAD: Me neither.

B1/MUM: I just don't get how some girls can be so...
Stupid.

B2/DAD: Stupid, stupid girl.

B1/MUM: So stupid.

HER: Yeh, OK! I get the message.

HIM: So she decides,
Not to run home?

B1: Not to tell her Mum.

...

What she needs is support

B2: Advice

B1: Someone to tell her **she`s** not done anything wrong

HIM: Can't she go to her pals?

B1 and B2 make a face.

B1: Oh, you mean the pals she's sort of, mostly dingyied for the
last year?

B2: The ones she didn't have as much time for once she met
Ryan?

B1: Got a job

B2: Started her Highers

B1: The pals that saw the pictures this morning
And said she probably did it for the attention?

HIM: ...People are shit.

...

B2: What about the guy with the glasses?

B1: The loner guy from reggie?

B2: He asked if she was OK

B1: He **did** reach out to Her...

B2: He seemed... kind?

B1: But she barely knows him

B2: But could he help Her?

B1 looks at HER. She considers it, then shakes her head.

B1: The sad fact is that for the last year,
she probably hung out with Ryan's pals more than her own.

B2: The very guys that sabotaged her

HIM: She should confront them then

B1: Are you out of your mind?!

B2: Go and speak to the guys who put her tits all over the
internet?

HIM: Why not?!

B1: The same guys who ping your bra straps for laughs?

HIM: Call it out then

B2: And make gay jokes when you pass in the corridor?

HIM: Stand up to them

B1: You want to send her into a room with those guys??

HIM: Well, challenge it!

B1: You challenge it!

Pause while HIM is forced to reflect a little. Then, a light bulb moment

HER: Periods happen!

B1: Ms French's lesson

HIM: The things nobody wants to talk about?

HER: Periods happen.
Young People Have Sex.

HER and B1: Consent Matters.

B2: But she can't remember the specifics

B1: She was looking at her phone waiting for Ryan to text

B2:   She can't quite grasp the wording

B1 coughs to get their attention, she's wearing her MS FRENCH glasses

B1/FRENCH: "It is against the law to produce, possess or share
explicit images of anyone under 18,
even if this is done consensually,
even if a child creates an explicit image of themselves."

HER: So all of it then.

B1/FRENCH: "It is against the law…"

HER: All of it actually totally illegal

B1/FRENCH: "To produce
To possess
To share…"

HER: But Ryan will just say I knew.
He'll say I agreed to it.

B1/FRENCH: "It is against the law…"

HER: I let him take one of me months back
I gave in and let him take it

B2:   Pressured consent,
is not consent.

B1:   And this time, he didn't even ask

HER: I should have made it clearer
Said no earlier

B2:   She couldn't have said 'no' earlier

B1:   She was asleep

HER: No means No

OTHER 3:   NO!

B1:   Only yes means yes!

B2:   Everything else
Means no

HIM: Maybe later

B1:   That's a no

HIM: I'm not sure…

B2: That's a no

HIM: Saying nothing because you can't speak?

B1, B2, HIM: That's a no!!

HER: Enough!
I need to speak to Miss French.

5. THE BASE

Suggested images on screen: An orange tape line—we're getting closer.

B2: So she walks up to her room
The furthest away classroom in the block

B1: Walking passed endless doors
that interrupt the continuous orange line

B2: The middle ground
You can walk here, but only if you're en route to some place else

B1: Only if you don't plan on stopping for help

B2: Only to find...

HER: ...It's empty.

B1&2: Ugh!

HER: That means...

B1: We know what that means

B2: We know where she is

B1: It's like a staff room for a single department

B1: A tiny cupboard of a room that they squeeze half a dozen teachers in
alongside anyone who's currently on detention

B1: All of them in this wee room

B2: Swarming around each other, like flies

B1: There's no privacy in there for anyone

B2: And guaranteed
They're all buzzing around the one teacher you need to speak to

HER: She sees me at the door.
Peeking through the gap in the wood.
She sees me and she goes,

B1 takes on MS FRENCH'S role.

B1/FRENCH: Are you coming in?

B2: Ugghhh!

HER: I nod.
I mean, I think I nod.

B2: She doesn't move though.
She puts her hand on the door
but thinks about bolting

HER: It's not like I don't want to go in...

B2 & B1/FRENCH: What do you need me to do?

HER: But my tongue kinda twists in my mouth
It expands and my brain somehow forgets how to form words

FRENCH: Tell me what you need
And I'll—

HER: And yes I am aware I am still peering at her through a crack in the door
And I feel her eyes searching for me
Trying to see the whole of me

FRENCH: Did you want me for something?

HER: But the thing is, so is everyone else in there
Faces of older teachers blinking at me through their bi-focals
And guys on detention, staring...

FRENCH: Do you need my help?

HER: I try and will her out the base with my eyes
Maybe she'll be able to see it in my face?
Maybe she will telepathically understand
Woman to woman
Girl to girl
But she just sits there
Trying to waft everyone else out the way
Trying to see my face through the other bodies

And I feel like it's been at least 60 seconds since I spoke
Or moved
Or blinked even
It's been at least a minute
And all of a sudden time is all I can think of
And the clock on the wall is all I can hear
And even when she stands
Even when she gets up from her chair and beckons me in
I can't go in there!

HER takes a breath, B1 removes her glasses.

I start to think about logistics.
Legalities.

B2: What if French is legally obliged to pass it on.

B1: What if she has to tell the Head.

B2: Her parents.

B1: The police?

HER: I think I might be sick
Or maybe I should pretend that I might be sick
So I have an excuse
So it looks less weird
So it looks like maybe I was just a bit ill

And so I cover my mouth
And I back away
I use my other hand to feel the way forward
And I run
And I run
And don't stop running
Until I'm outside
Until the fresh air hits me
It hits my throat and it turns out

She vomits.

B1 pulls HER's hair back, they walk in front of HER, leaving HER on the floor in the background.

B2: It's a while before we see her again at school.

B1: A good couple of weeks at least
For things to settle

B2: For the judgment and gossip to fade

B1: In the real world anyway

B2: Oh the pictures went round for months

B1: Bitchy comments and vulgar jokes
Bursting from the comments

B2: Or hiding in the DMs of folk pretending to be disgusted,
but still sharing the images

B1: Some folk were genuine
Some tried to reach out

B2: And it must work because fair play to her,
She comes back

B1: Looks like half the person she was though
Can you lose that much weight in a fortnight?

B2: You see, with a bit of distance

B1: With a bit of reflection

B2: The humiliation,
That sick, mortified feeling

B1: It soon made way for the realisation
that she was a victim now

B2: A victim of sexual abuse.

B1: That's the truth.
That's what it is

B2: And it's a hard pill to swallow

B1: Hits you like bus

B2: So when she comes back, She's a different version of herself

B1: One that's half numb,
half absolutely raging.

...

B2: Her Dad drives her in now
Makes sure that she goes through the front door

B1: Makes sure that she physically walks inside the entrance

B2: The main entrance that takes you past the Head's office
A blue room, protected
by red sticky tape

HIM appears in the shadows.

B1: She sees a familiar face, but she looks away

B2: She doesn't see Him coming out the Head's office

B1: Another warning

B2: After another fight

B1: She doesn't see His Stepdad walk out with Him

B2: She doesn't hear the Stepdad call out the Head for not looking out for 'his kid'

B1: Or the words his Stepdad tells Him as they leave

B2: The words that hit home
Words that unlock something inside of Him

B1: She doesn't see that finally,
Somebody has shown up for Him.
For the first time, since She tried to.

B2: She doesn't notice any of this
because just along the corridor from the entrance
is the common room

B1: The musty sweaty smell
Of boys' skin
And girls' body spray

B2: She's frozen to the spot when she sees it,
Her breath quickens and her hands turn to fists

B1: The room is empty
apart from that sofa.

B2: And even when she goes along to class
nobody notices

B1: Nobody sees how spaced out she is

B2: Teachers tell her off for not following along
for not keeping up

B2: She gets into trouble for being late to every class
and she doesn't care.

B1: Small price to pay for getting to walk down the halls on her own

B2: Avoiding everyone

B1: Avoiding Ryan

B2: Who is still very much here by the way

B1: Who is still at school, walking about, living his best life.

B2: And she thinks about leaving.
She thinks about giving in to the numb side

B1: But then She sees Him.

HIM appears again and He stops when He sees HER.

And He looks at Her like it's the first time He's seen her face.

B2: And He ignites something in Her
A fire starts to burn

B1: A fury like the one She used to see in Him
all those years ago when they were kids

B2: He's the only person who knows her

B1: Like really knows her

B2: Pals from before

B1: Since they were babies.

HE smiles. SHE tries to smile back but it doesnt show on her face.

B2: ...And maybe it's desperation

B1: Or maybe she's just ready to fight.

B2: If anyone could help Her

B1: If anyone **would** help Her

B2: Surely...

SHE moves like she's about to approach HIM, but He's already walking away

B1: Surely it would be Him?

6. THE PARTY

Suggested Images on screen: A line of green tape. A free for all. A place anybody can freely grace with their presence.

B2: A house party

B1: A gaff.

B2: Some girl in 6th Year

B1: When the parents go on holiday
The pals move in

B2: Supposed to be a small thing

B1: A gathering

B2: A catch up

B1: Definitely not a house party.

B2: It's totally a house party.
in one of those mental massive homes you get lost in
just going from the front door to the kitchen

B1: Bit risky for Her like
Word would spread like wildfire that she was there.

B2: But that was important

B1: That was important because then she only had to do this once.

...

B2: People often talk about the importance of timing

B1: When you tell a joke

B2: Confess something

B1: Deliver bad news.

B2: But **bad** timing

B1: A missed opportunity

B2: Can turn a pinnacle moment
into a complete shit show.

B1: And so she arrives and she sees Him right away
talking to some guy.

HIM is talking to B2, B2 becomes a random guy at the party, this guy is awful.
The actual worst. He lifts his collar up to show change of character.

B2/RANDOM: Aye, so I reckon if I can just
Starve ma self of water for a bit
It'll just
suck everything in

B1: She reconsiders when she sees who he is talking to

HIM: Starve yourself?

B1: This guy.

HIM: Do you mean dehydrate?

RANDOM: Aye

B1: A friend of Her now-ex
and the most likely culprit who spread the images of her around
the school.

HIM: You want to deliberately dehydrate yourself...?!

RANDOM: *(Lifts his shirt a little)* Gotta be serious if you want the abs.

B1: Nah. Too much at stake here.
She'll ask to speak to Him alone
Try and get Him out the room
She'll just have to—

RANDOM: See this lassie?

B1: And they tower over his phone

HIM: I don't know what I'm looking at

RANDOM: She's hot, eh?

B1: It's now or never
She walks in and stops.
She takes a deep breath
And she hears..

RANDOM: She's well fit now. Think how she'll look when she's—

HIM: Wait, she's...

B2: Aye she's 13 the now like,
But ye can just tell—

B1: Nope.
Nope. Nope. Nope. Nope. Nope. Nope. Nope. Nope.

HIM: She's thirteen??

HER leaves the space immediately.

B1: She's off.
Christ almighty He's become one of them

HER: I need to get out of here.

B1: And she feels stupid
Of course this was going to happen
Of course this is who he would become
Because isn't this guy
who every boy grows up to be?

HER tires to find the door but she's dizzy with all the people and music and she doesn't hear the end of the boys' conversation.

HIM: Are you serious??
Are you actually showing me the instagram of 2nd Year?

RANDOM: Tik Tok.

HIM: Whatever.

RANDOM: I mean...

HIM: She's a fucking child.

RANDOM: Aye now she's a child.
I mean like
Later...
Later when she's older
I'm just saying, like
I totally would

HIM: Would what?

HIM steals RANDOM's mobile.

RANDOM: Och. C'mon man!

HIM: Tell me.
What would you do to that 13-year-old lassie?

RANDOM: ...I mean.
Jesus!
When you say it it sounds pure rapey.

HIM: I think her big brother's in the next room,
Mon we'll find him and see what he reckons

RANDOM: Mate...

HIM: Nah, your clearly think it's OK, so

RANDOM: Alright, Christ, I'll delete it!

HIM: Too late, you've said it now.

RANDOM: I didn't mean it.

HIM throws the phone back. RANDOM reluctantly gets rid of the photos.

Right, See? Gone.

HIM: That's not right.

RANDOM: (*defensive*) ...Alright.

HIM: I'm out of here.

...

B1: And as He tries to leave, She's over here
In some kind of fight or flight mode

B2: But she can't seem to do either
Instead she just
Freezes.
Stuck to the carpet until...

B1 becomes random GIRL at party.

B1/GIRL: Guys are the worst.

HER: Sorry?

GIRL: Saw your pictures.

HER: I—

GIRL: Seen better to be honest.

HER: No... I didn't

GIRL: Take this

HER: I don't drink

GIRL: You do now.

GIRL clinks her drink into HER's.

HER follows GIRL to a sofa.

B2: And She sees something in this girl
An ally
A shared experience

So, for the moment at least,
She decides to stay

HER is visibly nervous at first but the more she drinks the more she relaxes.

HIM: And I see Her
Sat with a group of girls from the year above
Never thought in a million years
She'd be here
But there She is

She's almost smiling.
And for a moment
I see her like I used to.
Ponytail and a blunt fringe.
Sitting watching Batman cartoons.
I catch her eye
and the smile vanishes

HER looks around for the girls she met, but they've vanished, she drinks more.

HIM: And so I want to go over
But I need to get my words right

HER picks up a baseball cap and puts it on squint, she looks up and laughs, as though someone has put their hat on HER. She takes off her coat and throws it to the ground.

And this guy in a baseball cap has just rocked up
And he likes her
He definitely likes her
So I guess I just—

B2: Fake.

B1: So fake

B2: So obviously the fake "I'm going to get dunk and laugh lots so everyone thinks I'm fine"

B1: Everyone thinks I'm totally over it

B2: And it works

B1: Course it works

B2: Because she looks happy

B1: She's totally OK

B2: And everyone can plainly see that so...

They turn away from HER. They do nothing.

...

HIM: Mum's current guy.
The one that asks if I'm "cool" (double thumbs up!)

He's got a daughter.
Nice wee lassie. P7
I have to pick her up from school some Fridays.
It's summer so
she's dressed for the weather, eh.
Couple of weeks ago,
she walks out the gate, turns the corner
and this van hurls down the road.
Swerves in right close to the kerb,
winds down the window.
And an old guy leans out
and whistles.

Not like, for a dog
Not like for a warning
But for her.

This fully grown guy
with a bald head and shite stubble
winds down his window
to wolfwhistle at an 11-year-old school girl.

On the other side of the stage, HER reacts like the baseball cap person is being aggressive so she takes the cap off and throws it away. She picks up a man's shirt and dances with it. She puts it on.

And I go over this a few times in my head, right?
Summer dress.
Primary school
She's four and a half feet tall!
There's no way he thought—
No way he could have mistook her for...

And I'm raging, right
Not just because of what he's done
But because I wasn't quick enough to shout back
I wasn't quick enough to think.
And now he's speeding round the corner
and my jaw must be on the floor because she looks up at me
she shrugs and she goes
"Yeh,
they always do that."

Pause for a moment to let that land.

I know what she's grown up with.
This guy that spends his days texting me
Just to see how I'm doing?
I'm no even his kid!

I watch him raise that wee girl
and think
You are so much better than any of us.
Better than anything
I've ever seen.
And she's got that.
in house.
every day.
She is sensible and secure and loved because of him
and **still**...

On the other side of the stage, HER pulls glasses off someone up high and puts them on. Pretends she's struggling to see. She drinks more from the bottle and is becoming visibly drunker. She stumbles.

And I look at ma life.
I look at how things are working out for me

when I've had a conveyor belt of white van men,
of shite role models,
ploughing through my life
since I was eight.

And not just in ma house.
Not just walking down the street
They're online.
They're on tellie
In films
These ripped, macho, angry guys
That have been told they need to look hard
Save the world
Be strong
Be a dick
Be whatever you need to be to stay in control.
It's fucked up!

On the other side of the stage HER sees some men's shoes. She points and laughs at them. Removes her own shoes and puts on the men's shoes. She continues to dance, stumble, drink.

I thought She was lucky.
I thought She'd escaped it.

But here She is
In this situation
because of us.
Because it's comfortable, right?
It's just the order of things.

Isn't it great having all the power.
Knowing that nobody
is going to do a thing about it

Tell me,
How comfortable are you feeling right now?

On the other side of the stage, HER sits down and tries to steady herself, she picks up another drink. She tries to take off the shirt, shoes and glasses but it's too difficult. They won't come off. Or maybe she's just not trying hard enough. Nobody tries to help HER.

B2: (*Sarky*) It's great he got there, eh?

B1: 'Bout bloody time.

B2: (*checks invisible watch*) How much soul searching did that actually take??

B1: Shame it's not enough though.

B2: Shame it's just Him

B1: Shame it's not the hundred other folk she's come into contact with recently

B2: The Manager in Her restaurant, who just laughed when She's forced
to take money for booze

B1: The 'pals' that ignored her instead of seeing if she was OK

B2: The parents who can't see that girls are the victims here

B1: The teachers who didn't bother to ask why she was always late

B2: Falling behind

B1: Unable to focus

B2: The girls at the party who gave her a litre of cider then took off

B1: Or anybody that had the opportunity to call him out.

B2: Anyone that could have said,

HIM: Ryan Deans**

On the other side of the stage, The baseball cap returns. HER looks up at it. Puts it on. It falls over her eyes and she can't see.

B1: If only someone had said
his name is...

B1, B2, HIM: RYAN DEANS*

B2: And every single person at school who shared those photos of her

B1: Passed them along

B2: Who slut-shamed her

B1: Laughed behind her back

B2: Or right in her face

B1: Even those who just saw it

B2: Just looked for a moment
But then did nothing.

On the other side of the stage, HER stands, looks like she might have help standing.

She is walked away, covered in men's clothes. her own coat and shoes are left lying.

B2: The volume of people that could have stopped this

B1: The minor characters you probably didn't even focus on.
I'm talking about you.

B2: (*to the audience*) Aye, what did you do when you saw those photos??

Long Pause—no answer comes.

B2: Yeh. that's what I thought.

HER is being led to the top of the stairs, towards a bedroom door.

B1: Turns out you don't have to be the photographer

B2: Or the person that sent round that first picture

B1: You don't have to have broken the law
to be guilty.

B2: But you also don't have to be a superhero
to save the world.

*They draw attention to HER now walking up the stairs, she's almost at the top
They watch HER ascend the stairs*

B2: Imagine how this could have turned out

B1: Imagine if someone

B2: Anyone

B1: had just said—

HIM: I'm sorry!

HER stops, stares back at them downstairs.

B1 puts on her glasses and becomes MS FRENCH, B2 puts on his glasses and becomes YOUNG GUY.

I should have said something sooner.

I should have...

Like you tried to do

...for me.

...I'm sorry.

FRENCH: I am so sorry this has happened to you.

YOUNG GUY: How can I help you?

HIM: What do you need?

ALL 3:   Tell me what you need,
And I'll do it.

A moment. We hear the first 16 seconds of 'When the Party is Over' by BIllie Eilish.

As it plays, HER says nothing, but eventually, slowly, she shrugs all the boys' clothing off. As she does so, HIM walks towards HER without ascending the stairs. We think we're out of the woods, until the music stops, until it is silent again, until a new voice is heard from across the room.

B1 and B2 have removed their glasses.

B1:   I am her.
By the way.

...

The one you heard about.
That's me.
I am she.
I am...
Actually, I don't...
have a name
I guess.

HIM: Wait a minute

B1: I don't have an actual name
Like you do

HIM: What's happening?

B1: But it doesn't change the fact

HIM: No, we did this already.

B1: All you need to know is

HIM: Stop!

B1: I am Her.

HIM: Can we stop??

B1: She is me.
And you'll have heard this before,

B2: I am Her.

HIM: What is happening??

B2: The one you heard about.
That's me.
I am—

HIM: What's going on?!

HER: I'll be honest.
I'm sick of talking about it.

B2: Actually,
I don't have a name
I
guess.

HIM: I can't—

HER: Not a lot of people believe
The truth

B2: But she is me.

HIM: I can't do this again

B2/HER: I am Her.

HER: The one you heard about.
That's me.

Voice overs and images on the above screens come in: women, men, non-binary people, from all backgrounds, religions, cultures, abilities, reciting the lines below, they overlap with one another and result in a cacophony of voices (resembling the Me Too movement) while HIM races about the stage trying to work out why the story appears to be looping back around.

As the voices become louder and more populous, 'Let's go Round Again' by The Primitives (2014) (not the song you're thinking of!) plays on loop, louder and louder. The song and their voices remain in the background until the end.

VOICES: I am Her.
The one you heard about.
That's me.
I am she.
I don't have a name
I guess.
I don't have an actual name
Like you do.
But all that matters
All you need to know is
I am Her.

B1: And actually.

B2: I need your help.

HIM: Enough of this

B1,2 HER: ...
I need you
To help me.

HIM: ENOUGH!

Snap to blackout and silence.

END OF PLAY

NOTES

**Please check with teachers that there is no pupil called Ryan Deans in their school—if there is, his surname should be changed for the final scene where his full name is called out. (p46)

INFORMATION FOR STUDY

Question at the heart of the play:

How can you be the change you want to see in the world, when you feel like the world is fighting against you?

What we aim to show in this play:

We want to live in a world where:
* consent matters
* women are believed, not victimised
* inequality is stamped out
* misogyny and sexism are challenged

Suggested Questions for a post-show discussion:

1. How many people could have stepped in? When could this have happened?
2. What would you suggest they do/say in order to step in?
3. What would you say/do to HER?
4. What is the law regarding the sharing of indecent images of people under 18?
5. Why do the characters correct HER when she says No means No?
6. What does consent mean to you?
7. Whose language or actions in the play needed to be called out? (most will say Ryan, but actually there's loads. Obviously Ryan and the guys who shared the pictures. But also the girls. Including even HER when she makes a comment about HIS Mum. Important that the young people realise that we are all complicit in this, society has created these conditions, we've all contributed, but this means we all have the power to dismantle it.)
8. What do you think stops HIM and HER from just talking to each other?

9. Do you think HIM and Ryan have had a similar upbringing?
10. Do you think young men are more likely to speak up and challenge inappropriate language or behaviour if they feel they have a safe space to do this? What tools do you think young men need in order to speak up and challenge this sort of behaviour?

Reference the 4 Ds:

How to Respond to a person in distress:

DIRECT—Call out the behaviour, check they are OK. Doing this in a group is safer.

DISTRACT—find a subtle//creative way to intervene, distract attacker with conversation to de-escalate the situation.

DELEGATE—get someone else to step in if you don't feel safe doing it yourself (police, teacher, parent). But get the person's consent first.

DELAY—check in with them afterwards, let them know they are not alone.

REFERENCES

Rape Crisis Scotland

www.rapecrisisscotland.org.uk

Helpline: 08088 01 03 02

Scotland`s Domestic Abuse and Forced Marriage Helpline

www.sdafmh.org.uk/en

0800 027 1234

Womensaid

womensaid.scot

Shakti Women`s Aid

Help for black, minority, ethnic women, children and young people who are experiencing, or who have experienced, domestic abuse.

shaktiedinburgh.co.uk

Amina—Muslim Women Resource Centre

mwrc.org.uk

Samaritans Scotland

www.samaritans.org/scotland/samaritans-in-scotland

Call 116 123

Childline

www.childline.org.uk

800 1111

White Ribbon Scotland—Men Working to End Violence Against Women

www.whiteribbonscotland.org.uk

Zero Tolerance

www.zerotolerance.org.uk

Engender

www.engender.org.uk

She Scotland

www.shescotland.org.uk Education Pack

ALSO AVAILABLE FROM SALAMANDER STREET

All Salamander Street plays can be bought in bulk at a discount for performance or study. Contact info@salamanderstreet.com to enquire about performance licences.

BALISONG by Jennifer Adam
ISBN: 9781914228377

Balisong is a play written for schools as part of the No Knives Better Lives Programme promoting positive and active citizenship among young people.

LOVE BITES by Sam Siggs
ISBN: 9781914228391

Midsummer night's eve in Edinburgh. A girl with wings and a plastic bow and arrow sits sobbing on a bench.
It's been a hard day. Love. Bites.

STORM LANTERN by Duncan Kidd
ISBN: 9781738429370

Caught by the Nazis distributing forbidden leaflets, Sophie Scholl is facing execution. Only one route remains: confession and betrayal of everything she stood for... but will she take it? What would you be willing to die for?

A Play, A Pie and A Pint Volume Two
ISBN: 9781068696237

8 plays from Òran Mór, celebrating 20 years of Glasgow's lunchtime theatre phenomenon, including critically acclaimed plays and favourites as voted by the public and members of the theatre company.

MASKING by Nina Lemon
ISBN: 9781738429318

Nina Lemon's insightful play sensitively explores the challenges faced by a group of school kids as they cope with a high-stakes school system in a world that's piling on the pressure.